IT'S LIKE WE TOUCHED THE MOON

BETH HOLLAR GIER

An imprint of Enslow Publishing

WEST **44** BOOKS™

Please visit our website, www.west44books.com.
For a free color catalog of all our high-quality books,
call toll free 1-800-398-2504.

Cataloging-in-Publication Data

Names: Gier, Beth Hollar.
Title: It's like we touched the moon / Beth Hollar Gier.
Description: Buffalo, NY : West 44, 2026. | Series: West 44 MG verse
Identifiers: ISBN 9781978597938 (pbk.) | ISBN 9781978597921 (library
bound) | ISBN 9781978597945 (ebook)
Subjects: LCSH: Coming of age--Juvenile fiction. | Camp--Juvenile
fiction. | Space--Juvenile fiction. | Apollo 11 (Spacecraft)--Juvenile fiction.
| Social action--Juvenile fiction.
Classification: LCC PZ7.1.G547 It 2026 | DDC [F]--dc23

First Edition

Published in 2026 by
Enslow Publishing
2544 Clinton Street
Buffalo, NY 14224

Editor: Caitie McAneney
Designer: Tanya Dellaccio Keeney

Photo Credits: Cover (background) 3d_kot/Shutterstock.com.

All rights reserved. No part of this book may be reproduced in any form
without permission in writing from the publisher, except by a reviewer.

Printed in the United States of America

CPSIA compliance information: Batch #CS26W44: For further information contact
Enslow Publishing LLC at 1-800-398-2504.

*For Libby and Onni:
Always remember you can touch the moon.
And for anyone who
has ever had to do
something that felt
WAY
TOO
HARD.*

SUMMER 1969

They named me after
Princess Grace.
Not knowing I would
fall for space.

That Grace is a
movie star, with
fancy gowns and
long black cars.

But I like stars of
other kinds.
Stars that shimmer.
Stars that shine.

Astronauts, and
planets, moons.
These are things that
make me swoon.

If I could meet
her highness Grace?
I would suggest
she check out space.

ON WARM SUMMER NIGHTS

when I was small,
    Dad and I would sit
    side by side
    in the cool grass.

Study the sky.

Sometimes we got lucky and
    spotted a
    shooting star.

Make a wish, Grace,
    Dad would say.

I want to touch the moon,
    I would whisper.

You can do anything you want to,
    Dad would say.

        And I believed him.

IT'S THE LAST DAY OF SEVENTH GRADE

The science room
      feels like an oven.

Mr. Brodie slaps tests
      down on desks.

Not bad—for a girl,
      he says,
      when he gets to mine.

Even though I got an A+.
Like always.

Brodie thinks it's silly that
      I want to be an
      astronaut.

That's a man's job,
      he always says.
      Everyone knows that.

And then he laughs.

Real funny, Brodie.
      Real funny.

Finally the bell rings
        and we stream out.

A new flyer
        posted in the hallway
        catches my eye.

Maple Grove Recreation Department

SPACE CAMP
Meet a Real NASA Scientist!
Watch the Moon Walk with us!

July 19-20, 1969
White Pines Boy Scout Camp

Outstanding science students in grades 7-9 should apply by filling out the form below and returning to Mr. Brodie in person or by mail.

Name:
Grade:
Address:
Phone:
Math grade average:
Science grade average:

Someone has written
>   **TAKE ONE!**
>   across the flyer
>   in red ink.

I pull a copy
>   from the stack
>   pinned to the board.
Head outside.

Denise is waiting
>   for me
>   on the corner
Like always.

We've been best friends
>   since we were four.
Sharing snacks
>   on the patio.

I don't even remember
>   how we met.

It's like we've
>   ALWAYS
>   been close.

I show Denise the flyer.

Look at this!
> I say.
> *Wouldn't it be far out to watch the moon walk . . . ?*

But I can tell
> she's not really
> listening to me.

Instead, she waves
> to a boy
> across the street.

Flashes a smile.

Tosses her shiny, dark hair.

I sigh.

Tuck the flyer
> back into my notebook.

Lately it seems like
> Denise would rather
> hang out with the
> cool kids.

It's funny how
        I can't remember
        the beginning of
        our friendship.

But somehow
        I'm starting to
        imagine
              the
                      end.

THE HOUSE IS WIDE OPEN

But Cyndy's door is shut tight.

Her music is
      turned up
      LOUD.
thump, thump, thump

Like always.
    ♪ *Smoke on the water . . .* ♪
thump, thump, thump

Mom is sitting on the couch,
    sipping a Tab,
    reading the newspaper.
Like she has every day since
    Dad left for
    Vietnam.

Her gray eyes have
    shadows under them.

We have the same red hair,
    but hers looks dull.
thump, thump, thump

Mom can't get enough of the news.

Or the tiny pills
    the doctor gave her to
    help her relax.

thump, thump, thump

I go to my room.

thump, thump, thump

Pull out the Space Camp flyer.

thump, thump, thump

Fill out the form.

thump, thump, thump

Mom gives me a stamp.

I bike to the post office.

Drop everything
    into the mailbox.

And then
    I WAIT.

thump, thump, thump

I keep a box
behind my shoes.
It's made of cardboard,
painted blue.

The box protects
my space-y stuff.
Mom thinks I have
quite enough.

But NASA just keeps
sending things!
Planet posters,
postcards, pins.

Apollo patches,
pencils, pens, and
one signed photo
of John Glenn.

If someone asks you
"Where is Grace?"
Chances are I'm
lost in space.

EVERY NIGHT AT 6:00

Mom turns on the news.
The guy who reports it
    always sounds
    low, steady, calm.

Like someone you can trust.

Mom leans in
    when they show Vietnam,
    looking for Dad.
We haven't seen him yet.
But we keep watching
    night after
        night after
            night.
And the guy is always
    low, steady, calm.

Funny thing is
    I NEVER feel
    low, steady, calm
    when I'm watching
    news from Vietnam.

Not even close.

THE NEXT AFTERNOON

Denise comes by.

We're biking to the beach.

There's a bunch of people going,
    Denise says.
    I hope Kevin comes.

Who's Kevin?
    I ask.

But we set off
    on the hilly ride
    through the dunes
    before she can
    answer.

By the time we get there,
    the group has gathered.

We spread our bright towels
    on the cool sand,
    baby oil
    on our winter-pale skin.

The sun is gentle,
> just warm enough to
> soften the chilly air.

I walk to the edge of the water.
It laps at my feet
> and it's
> ICE COLD.

The sun may say
> SUMMER.
But Lake Michigan still says
> WINTER.

When I get back to my towel,
> everyone's up,
> talking.

Anyone going to Brodie's Space Camp?
> someone asks.
> *Or should I say, dork camp?*

They all crack up.

I almost say,
I am!
But I stop myself.

Denise speaks up
      instead.
Grace is going! Right, Grace?

Everyone looks at me.

I'm sure my face is
      bright
      red.

I glare at her.
Thanks a lot, Denise,
      I say.
(But only to myself.)

I was right.

Things ARE
      changing.

And I don't like it.

EVERY SUNDAY

we go to church.

Every Sunday
    I say a prayer for Dad.

Every Sunday
    I look around at the
    packed pews.

Every Sunday
    I wonder about
    all those people with their
        heads bowed
        hands folded.

Do they
    pray for him,
    too?

Every Sunday?

My dad is stuck
in Vietnam. It's
just my sister,
me, and Mom.

Left behind to
do our best.
It's very hard.
We're all distressed.

Cyndy's music
gets her through.
Mom has her pills.
I have the moon.

We watch TV.
We count the days,
until he's home with
us to stay.

Until he walks right
through that door.
I really hate this
stupid war.

WE GET LETTERS FROM DAD

every week.

I love reading Dad's letters.
Even though they
    make me
      miss him more.

Mom says
    he'll be home in
    August.

That this is
    his last tour.

That he is
    too old to be
    called up
    again.

I just hope
    she's right.

I just hope
    he makes it to
    August.

ONE WEEK LATER

I'm
        still
                waiting.

I try to keep busy,
        but the hot days
        draaaaaaag
        on and on.

Then FINALLY—
        just when I'm about to give up—
        the letter arrives.

I rip it open.

Dear Grace,
Thank you for your interest in Space Camp . . .

And then there's a
        list of 10 names.

THEY
ARE
ALL
BOYS.

I read the letter again,
    just to be sure I'm not
    missing something.

THERE
ARE
NO
GIRLS.

This CAN'T be right.

Maybe I made a
    mistake
    on the form?

Maybe they made a
    mistake
    on the list?

I don't know
    what went wrong.

But I do know this:
    I am going to find out.

I PICK UP
THE PHONE

Stretch the curly cord as
    loooooong as it will go.

Around the corner.
Into the hallway.

My hand shakes
    as I dial.

Recreation Department!
    a woman chirps.
    How can I help you?

I clear my throat.

Um, hi,
    I say.
    There's been a mistake.

I describe the problem
    as calmly as I can.

And there are NO GIRLS on the list,
    I say, finally.

Let me check with the boss,
>says the woman.
>*Be right back.*

I hear heels
>*click-click-clicking*
>on a hard floor.

A door opening with a
>*squeeeeak.*

Closing again with a
>*thunk.*

A few minutes later,
she comes back.

Hello?
>she says.
>*My boss said they couldn't find
>a female chaperone.
>So they made the camp boys only.*

They couldn't find anyone?
>I ask.
>*Did they even try?*

My voice is louder now.

I understand why you're upset,
    the woman says.
    I'm very sorry.

But we do have a nice
    baton twirling class you might enjoy,
    she says.
    It meets on . . .

I hang up.
    HARD.

Breathing.
    HARD.

Why does everything
    have to be
    so
    HARD?

CYNDY COMES IN

What are you all mad about?
> she asks, combing fingers through
> her long, blond hair.

I tell her about the letter.

She wrinkles her
> freckled nose.

What did you expect, Grace?
> she shrugs.
> *You're not surprised, are you?*

<SIGH>

A few minutes later,
> Mom gets home.

She pops open a Tab.

Swallows one of her
> tiny yellow pills.

I tell her about the letter.

I'm sorry, Gracie. Life isn't fair,
    she sighs.
    But you know that already.

        <SIGH>

I call Denise and
    tell her about the letter.

Well, look at it this way,
    she says.
    *Maybe this is a sign you should try
    something less dorky.*

I don't say anything.

Grace? Helloooo? Are you there?
    Denise says.

Yeah I'm here,
    I say.
    I gotta go.

        <SIGH>

I hang up and go to my room.

Flop down on my bed.

Can't they see how
      UNFAIR
      this is?

I'd give anything to
      talk to Dad.

I know he'd understand.

But White Birch, Michigan,
      is more than
      8,000 miles
      from Vietnam.

I'll just have to do
      the best I can
      without him.

I'M STILL THINKING ABOUT DAD

when I have an idea.

I pull out a fresh sheet of
  notebook paper.

At the top
  I write:

PETITION

Below that,
  I write:

WE BELIEVE
girls should be allowed to attend Space Camp.

WE BELIEVE
the decision to exclude them should be reversed.

Below that
  I write:

NAME   **ADDRESS**   **SIGNATURE**

I'll show them.

I may not look it, but
    I am tough.

I'll get
    EVERYONE I know
    to sign
    my petition.

They are
    NOT going to
    get away with this.

The news is out.
It's very clear that
girls are just not
welcome here.

Boys with average
grades are in.
But girls with excellent
marks can't win.

It drives me batty.
Makes me mad!
I feel as though I
have been had!

'Cause it's no secret:
Girls are just
as smart as boys.
But still they must:

Push their way in.
Fight to be heard.
I'm going to fix this.
Mark my word.

THE NEXT MORNING

I stuff the petition
   into my pocket.

Ride my bike to
   Mrs. Green's house.

She teaches English
   at my school.

Would you proofread something for me?
   I ask.

And then I tell her
   everything.

Of course,
   she says when I've finished.

Her eyes move
   left >>> to >>> right >>> as >>> she >>> reads.

When she's finished,
   she sighs.

This is excellent, Grace,
    she says.
    And I have an idea.

Mrs. Green tells me
    she will serve
    as a chaperone.

Add that to your petition,
    she says.
    Then they'll have no excuses.

You'd do that?
    I say.

I'd be happy to, Grace,
    says Mrs. Green.
    Now—you need to get to work!
    You can do it, Grace!

        And I believe her.

I PULL MOM'S OLD TYPEWRITER

from the hall closet.
Set it up on the
    kitchen table.

I love the smell of the
    inked-up ribbon.
    The sound of the bell *ding-dinging,*
    telling me it's
    time for a
    new line.
    The sharp *putch-putch-putch*
    of the keys
    hitting the roller.
    The *scratchy ratchet-y racket*
    when I pull out the paper.

It's finished.
I'm ready.

I carefully sign
    on the first line:
    Grace Kelly Donovan

I smile.
That's one!

TODAY'S THE DAY

I need 40 signatures
      to get them to
      change their minds.

Mom and Cyndy are
      sleepy-eyed when I
      slide the petition
      across the kitchen table.

It's ready!
      I say.
      Here's a pen!

Mom sips her coffee.
Scribbles her name on
      line two.

She pushes the petition
      back across the table.
Smiles faintly.

Good luck, honey,
      she says.

Cyndy sighs,
>	then signs.

She draws tiny hearts
>	in the Y's in her name.

There,
>	she yawns.

I find an extra pen
and a
>	clipboard.

See you later!
>	I call.

The screen door
>	claps shut
>	behind me.

I take a deep breath.

You can do this,
>	I tell myself.

I start down the sidewalk.

FIRST STOP IS MRS. FROST

I ring the bell.

Hi, Mrs. Frost,
    I say.
    Would you like to sign my petition?

I hold it up for her to see.

Explain the situation.

Of course I would!
    Mrs. Frost says.
    Come in, Grace.

Her flowy purple housedress
    swishes
        as she walks.

I breathe in roses and lavender.

Mrs. Frost's tiny poodle,
    Celeste,
        nips at my ankles.

Mrs. Frost goes to find
    her favorite pen.

She returns with
    that and
    a tin of
    oatmeal cookies.

Take these, Grace,
    she says.
    You need to keep up your strength.

She signs with a smile.

Pats me on the shoulder.

Opens the door.

It's a waning gibbous moon!
    she says.
    Perfect time for something like this!

Thanks, Mrs. Frost,
    I call from the sidewalk.

A waning gibbous moon?

I'm not sure
 what she's
  talking about.

But I have four signatures.
What's another 36?

I CAN do this.

I KNOCK ON A LOT OF DOORS

Hello!
    I begin, every time.

I always smile.

I'm Grace. Have you heard about the Space Camp?

About half of them
    end up signing.
They smile back.
Tell me to
    keep up the
    good work.

The other half
    won't sign.
They won't smile, either.
They tell me I should
    leave things alone.

But I don't let anyone
    get me down.

This is too
    important.

WHEN I GET HOME

the phone is ringing.

It's Denise.

A bunch of us are bowling tonight.
 Want to come?
 Denise asks.

I ask Mom.
She says it's okay.

I can go,
 I say.
 And I'll bring my petition so you can sign it.
 I'll ask the others, too.

Umm—maybe we could do that another time?
 says Denise.
 Let's just have fun tonight, Gracie! Okay?

But something about
 the way Denise says that
 makes me feel
 NOT
 okay.

39

When I get to the bowling alley,
    Denise is waiting
    at the door.

I see a kid
    I don't recognize
    working at the counter.

Who's that?
    I whisper.

His name is Dougie,
    Denise whispers back.
    He just moved here.
    He's our age.

She giggles.

He's a total dork.

I give Dougie
    my 55 cents.

He gives me my shoes.

Asks if I need help
    finding a ball.

His glasses are
> steamed up and
> he wipes them off
> on his shirt.

Definitely a dork.

But he seems nice.

Once everyone arrives,
> we get two lanes
> next to each other.

For the next three hours we
          and   and
laugh   laugh   laugh.
          and   and

It feels so good to laugh.

For three hours,
> I forget about everything.

Even Dad.

When I realize it later,
      I
       feel
       terrible.

But I can't
      think about Dad
     all the time.

Can I?

THE NEXT DAY AFTER LUNCH

I walk over to Denise's.
Ring the bell.

Denise answers.
Looks at me
      through the screen.

Hi, Grace. What's happening?
      she says.

I hold up the petition.
Want to sign?

Her eyes dart down and
      to the side.

And then Kevin
      is standing behind her.
He puts his hand on
      her shoulder.

It'll only take a minute . . .
      I begin.

But Denise interrupts me.

*Why don't you
 come back later, Grace?
 When I'm not so . . .*

She opens her eyes
 wide.
Jerks her head
 toward Kevin.

 . . . busy?

Umm . . . okay?
 I say.
But . . .

And I'm pretty sure my
 mouth is
 hanging open when
 Denise says,
I'll call you later, Grace!

And she closes the door
 in
 my
 face.

WE'RE GOING TO THE BEACH!

Mom announces
    when I get home.

I raise my eyebrows at Cyndy.

Mom hasn't been
    interested in
    fun things lately.

But she already has the
    beach bags and towels
    in the car.

Cyndy sits in front with Mom.
I take the back.

It's hot so we
    crank the windows
    all the way down.

I lean back against the
    sticky plastic seat.

Let the breeze cool my
    sweaty face.

Cyndy turns on the radio and
> we all sing along.
Even Mom.

Mom parks and
> we unload our stuff.

We're trudging through the sand,
> looking for a spot, when
> I see the new kid
> from the bowling alley.

Just when I think he's
> going to walk by
> without noticing me,
> he stops.

Weren't you at the bowling alley the other night?
> he asks, squinting.

Yeah, I say.
I cross my arms
> over my chest.
I'm Grace.

It's nice to meet you, Grace,
    he says, smiling.
    I'm Dougie.

We talk for a minute.

Well, see you around!
    I say.

I find Mom and Cyndy.

Who was that?
    Cyndy asks.

He's a new kid,
    I say.
    I met him at the bowling alley.

Huh,
    she says.
    He looks like a dork.

So what?
    I say.
    He's nice.

Cyndy doesn't answer.

Stretches out on
       her towel.

I stand in the sand.

Gaze at the waves.

Think about the
       infinite
       deep
       blue
       possibilities.

Almost as endless as the
       dark
       velvet
       night
       sky.

My mother has these
yellow pills.
She'll take them
every day until

my dad gets back from
Vietnam.
Meanwhile, they will
keep her calm.

Mom never cries or
lashes out.
That's what the pills
are all about.

I know they help her
to relax.
But shouldn't she—
somehow—react?

If I could
gather up the will,
I'd throw away
those yellow pills.

WHEN I GET UP THE NEXT DAY

there's a note
       from Mom
       on the kitchen table.

She wants me to
       pick up her pills
       at the drugstore.

On my way out
       after lunch,
       I grab the petition.

Denise's house is on the way.

I'll try again to
       get her to sign.

I pull my bike up next to
       their garage door,
       ring the bell.

Denise's mom answers
>	right away.

Grace!
>	she says.
>	*Come in, dear.*
>	*Denise! Grace is here!*

Denise comes out of her room.

Hey, Grace,
>	she says.
>	*What's happening?*

I brought the petition,
>	I say.
>	*I only need two more signatures.*
>	*I'll ask your mom, too.*
>	*Here.*

I hold out the
>	paper and a pen.

But Denise doesn't take them.

She looks at the floor.

Grace, you're gonna be mad at me,
    she says finally.

What do you mean?
    I ask.
    Why would I be mad at you?

She sighs.

Look, Grace,
    she says.
    I can't sign your petition.

For a second I think
    I heard her wrong.

What are you talking about?
    I ask.

Denise stands up straighter.
Looks at me.

I'm not going to sign,
    she says.
    Maybe girls shouldn't go to Space Camp, actually.

What are you talking about?
    I ask again.

Well, Kevin says . . .
    Denise begins.

Kevin?
    I say, louder than I expect.
    What does Kevin have to do with this?

I'm still holding the paper
    out for her to take.

My face burns.

I'm sure you'll find two more people to sign,
    Denise says finally.

Her voice trails off.

I don't know what to say.

All I know is
    I need to
    get out of here
    before I cry.

I push the door open.

Take some
>deep
>breaths.

It's fine, it's fine, it's fine, it's fine . . .
>I tell myself
>over and over.

But it's not fine.

Denise is
>supposed to be
>my best friend.

How can this be
>happening?

I FEEL HEAVY, WEIGHED DOWN

But somehow
    I make it to the drugstore.

I prop my bike up
    in the rack.

A tiny silver bell
    jangles when
    I open the door.

I make my way to the
    back of the store.
Past shelves full of
    Chuckles and clove gum and candy cigarettes.

Hi there, Grace. Picking up for your mom?
    the pharmacist asks.

I just nod.
I know if I try to talk,
    I'll cry.

He pulls a
    small bottle from
    under the counter.

Drops it into a
>	waxy white bag.

I hand him the money
>	Mom left me.
He smiles.
Counts out the change.

Just as I turn to go,
>	the bell on the door
>	rings again.
I see Dougie and someone
>	who must be his mom
>	coming my way.

She's short, like me.
She wears glasses, like Dougie.

Dougie smiles when he sees me.

Hi, Grace!
>	he says.
>	*Grace, this is my mom. Mom, this is Grace.*

I force a smile.

It's nice to meet you, Grace,
    she says.

What are you up to?
    Dougie asks.

Well,
    I say.

And then I tell them the
    whole story.

They listen.
Nod.

They're having a NASA scientist speak,
    I say.
    I would give ANYTHING to hear him talk.

No one says anything
    for a second.

Well, Grace . . .
    Dougie's mom says.
    I would love to sign your petition.

Me, too, Grace,
    Dougie says.

Dougie's mom reaches
        into her purse,
           pulls out a pen.

I spread the petition
        flat
           on the counter.

They read it over.

Then they both sign.

I really hope you can go,
        Dougie says.
        Let me know what happens.

Come on, Douglas,
        says Dougie's mom.
        Let's find those Band-Aids we need.
        Good luck, Grace!

I watch them as they go.

Not quite believing what
        just happened.

I'm still
>   really
>   mad
>   at Denise.

But I don't care as much
>   as I did
>   before.

Because I have
>   40 signatures!

Time to deliver
>   this thing to the
>   Recreation Department.

THERE'S A WOMAN SITTING

at a desk in the lobby.

She looks up at me.
How can I help you?
    she asks.

I'm dropping off a petition,
    I say, handing it to her.

Her eyes grow wide
    as she looks at the
    list of names.

My goodness!
    she says.
    You have been busy!
    I will be sure to pass this on.

And suddenly I feel different.
    Lighter.
    Much lighter.

Maybe
    even
        hopeful.

MOM GETS HOME AT 3:30

looking tired.

Did you get my pills, Grace?
    she asks.

They're in the cupboard by the sink,
    I say.
    I turned in the petition today.

Good for you, honey,
    Mom says.

She doesn't ask
    any questions.

She doesn't ask
    how I'm feeling.

She just finds her pills,
    grabs her Fresca.

Drops onto the couch.

Opens her newspaper.

If Dad were here,
    he'd want to know
    all the details.

If Dad were here,
    he'd ask
    lots and lots of
    questions.

If Dad were here,
    he
    would
    care.

A COUPLE DAYS LATER

I'm finishing my Froot Loops
    when the phone rings.

I hurry to pick it up.

Hope it's someone
    calling with good news
    about Space Camp.

Hello? Donovan residence. Grace speaking,
    I say.

Hi, Grace. This is Dougie.

Oh. Hi,
    I say.

I hope I don't sound too
    bummed out.

I'm biking to the beach today,
    Dougie says.
Want to come?

We agree to meet
        by the school
        in an hour.

I hang up,
        shake my head.

If someone told me
        a week ago
        that Denise and I would
        not be talking.

That I'd be riding my bike
        to the beach
        with the new kid
        named Dougie.

I would not have believed it.

But it's been a *strange* summer.

And it
        just
        keeps
        getting
                stranger.

DOUGIE
AND I PEDAL

through the dunes
    to the beach.

We lean our bikes on some
    weathered wooden benches.

Sit down in the sand.

The beach is empty today.

It's cloudy and
    the water is steel gray.

The waves are the
    biggest I've seen
    in a while.

So you really dig the space stuff, huh?
    Dougie asks.

Yeah. My dad got me into it,
    I say.

Did he help you with the petition?
    he asks.

Um, no. He's not here,
>I say.
>>*He's in Vietnam.*

We stare at the lake.

That must be hard,
>says Dougie.

Yeah, it is,
>I say.
>>*Moving must be hard, too.*

I guess,
>Dougie shrugs.
>*I'm adjusting.*
>*But there's something I . . .*

CRACKLE-flash-CRACKLE

Lightning zigzags
>across the sky.

BOOM-boom-BOOM

Thunder rumbles
>right behind.

We jump on our bikes, but
        we don't get far before
        the storm lets loose.

It rains so hard
        it stings
        when the drops
        hit my arms.

It's hard to see
        where I'm going.

When we get to the corner,
        Dougie yells,
Turning this way! See you later!

I coast into the garage,
        grab a beach towel from
        the hook on the wall.

Dry myself off.

Shivering and smiling
        at the same time.

I go inside and stretch out on
       the couch.

Wrap myself in a blanket.

       Think about
       how nice
       it is to
       have a new
       friend.

Think about
       how maybe "strange"
       isn't so bad
       after all.

NEXT THING I KNOW

the phone is ringing again.

I stand up too fast.

See stars.

I pick up the phone.

Hello?
    I croak.

Yes, hello. Grace Donovan, please,
    says a man's gruff voice.

Uh . . . this is Grace,
    I say.

I blink myself awake.

Hello, Grace.
    the voice says.
    I'm calling to let you know . . .

It's the Rec Department director.

He's calling to tell me
> they've changed their minds.

I can go to Space Camp!

As long as Mrs. Green is there at ALL times,
> he says.

He hangs up with a click.

I just stand there
> for a minute.

Let the good news
> soak in.

I did it!
> I say out loud, even though
> no one is around
> to hear it.

**I
DID
IT
!!!**

IT'S FUN TO SHARE GOOD NEWS

for a change.

I tell Mom.
I'm proud of you, Grace,
        she says.

I tell Cyndy.
Far out, Grace!
        she says.

I tell Mrs. Green.
It's going to be great, Grace!
        she says.

I tell Mrs. Frost.
The waning gibbous moon never fails, Grace,
        she says.

I tell Dougie.
That's groovy, Grace!
        he says.

Finally, I write a letter to Dad.
You can touch the moon, Grace.
      he'd whisper.

If only he were here.

It feels so good to
finally win! To
celebrate that
girls are in!

It shouldn't have to
be this way.
Petitions really
aren't the way

to make things fair
and square and right.
We shouldn't have to
argue, fight.

But back to
celebrating-wow!
I really couldn't
be more proud!

And when they
wonder about space?
The boys will say,
"Let's just ask Grace."

IT'S THE FOURTH OF JULY

Cyndy leaves early to
>   meet up with her friends
>   before the fireworks.

Have fun!
>   I say, as she pushes the screen door open.

She scowls.
Lets the door slam.

LOUD.

Mom and I pack
>   blankets and
>   bug spray and
>   brownies
>   in the
>   big orange
>   beach bag.

Mrs. Frost walks over at
>   just the right time.

We pile into the car and
>   head for the park.

It's already crowded
>	by the time we get there.
But we find a spot to
>	spread out our blankets.

It's getting dark when
>	I spot Denise.

We've always gone to the
>	fireworks together.
Until now.

She's making her way
>	through the crowd
>	with Kevin
>	at her side.

I wonder if
>	she'll come over.
Say hi.

She doesn't.

I lie back on the blanket.

Try to pretend that
      I don't care about
           Denise.

But it's harder
      than I thought
      it would be.

IT'S RAINING AGAIN

I climb into bed.

I leave my window open
    so I can hear it
    bounce off the roof.

Run through the
    gutters to the
    downspouts.

Soon I'm dreaming.

Dougie's there, and
    Mrs. Frost.

We're in our backyard
    looking at a model of
    the Apollo 11 rocket.

You do the countdown, Grace,
    they say.

10, 9, 8 . . .
    I say.

And the rocket blasts off.
Everyone cheers and claps.

                  clap, clap, clap
                  thump, clap, clap
                  thump, thump, clap

thump, thump, thump

I open my eyes,
        confused.

thump, thump, thump

Cyndy's music is LOUD.

thump, thump, thump

I pull my pillow
        over my head.

thump, thump, thump

I'm too tired to
        get up to
        ask her to turn it off.

thump, thump, thump

So the music keeps playing.

thump, thump, thump

And I try hard

thump, thump, thump

to ignore

thump, thump, thump

the words.

Something about a bad moon rising.
Something about trouble on the way.

IT'S ANOTHER MUGGY NIGHT

The cicadas are
      buzzing like
         extra-busy bees.

Mom and I are watching
      Let's Make a Deal.

We have the front door
      wide open.
Wishing for a
      wisp of cool air.

There's a knock and
      I get up.

Mrs. Green is
      standing on the porch.

Hi, Grace,
      she says.

Her face is pale and
      her eyes are red
         around the edges.

Can I come in?
    she asks.

Yeah, of course,
    I say, holding the screen door open.

Mom is up now, too.

Hi Nancy,
    she says.
    Everything okay?

Mrs. Green comes in.
Falls into Dad's chair.
Wipes her nose
    with a tissue.

I have bad news,
    she says.

What's wrong?
I ask.

Grace, I'm so sorry,
she begins.

Her voice is shaky.

I know you're counting on me,
        she says.
           But I need to go to Iowa.
           My mother is very sick.

Now she's crying.

The doctors don't think she has much time . . .

Is this really happening?

Maybe it's just a bad dream?
        Or a bad joke?

I know that I should say
        something nice.

Something kind.

Something encouraging.

But I don't.

I just stand there.

Mom murmurs to
        Mrs. Green.
Rubs her shoulder.

I'm so sorry, Nancy,
        she says.
        It'll be okay.

I swallow hard,
        bite my tongue,
          try to stay quiet.

Now Mom is rubbing
        my shoulder.

Grace, I know . . .
        Mom says.

I jerk away from her.

Go to my room,
        close the door.

Crawl into bed
        in my clothes.

The moon
      is shining
      WAY
      TOO
      BRIGHT
through my window.

Like it's making fun of me.

Stupid moon.

Doesn't it understand how

DARK

things are
right now?

IT'S NOT SUNDAY

But after breakfast,
    I ride my bike to the
    church anyway.

It's empty.
And musty and damp
    from all the rain.

I slide into a
    hard,
    worn-smooth bench
    in the back.

I start with the
    usual prayer for Dad.

Then I say a prayer for
    Mrs. Green's mom.

That she'll be
    cured.

That Mrs. Green can
    come to camp
    after all.

I know that last part is
	selfish.

But I can't help it.

I don't even know
	what else to
	pray for,
	to be honest.

So amen, I guess,
	I say, standing up.
Amen.

I TAKE THE LONG WAY HOME

Past the lake.

It's warm and windy.

The beach is already
    swarming with swimmers.

White-capped waves
    roll in fast,
    crash onto the shore, then
    retreat.

I collapse into the sand
    under a scrawny pine tree.
The dune grass surrounds me,
    whispering.

I look out at the water.

What if Dad were just
    over there?
Across the lake?

What if I could swim to him?

It catches me by surprise
        when I start to
        cry.
I don't even feel it coming.

I pull up my knees,
        bury my face in them so
        no one will see me.

I cry for a
        really long time.
Hard.

Until I'm completely
        empty.

Finally I get up,
        brush the sand off.

Trudge back
        to my bike.

I'm so exhausted that
        halfway up the
        long hill
        I stop and walk.

A loud car full of
        high school kids
        passes me
        too close.

They lean out the windows.
Laugh like
        me pushing my bike
        up the hill
        is hilarious.

I don't even care.

Let them laugh.

It's not like things can
        get any worse.

DOUGIE CALLS RIGHT AFTER LUNCH

We visited my grandparents over the weekend,
    he says.

That's nice,
    I say.

But I know I don't
    sound nice.

I sound frustrated.

How are you?
    Dougie asks.
    Getting ready for camp?

I sigh.

Tell him the
    long
        sad
            story.

So no Space Camp for me.
    I say, finally.

I wait for Dougie to
    say something
      nice.
Something
    encouraging.

But all he says is,
I gotta go, Grace. I'll call you later, okay?
    and hangs up.

I stand there.

Stare at the phone in my hand.

Maybe things can
    get worse.

Maybe they just did.

I DON'T KNOW
WHAT ELSE TO DO

So I call Denise.

Hello? Denise answers.

Hi, it's Grace,
    I say.

Grace? Oh! Hi!
    Denise says.
    What's happening?

She sounds surprised.

Not much,
    I say.
    Want to come over?
    Listen to music or something?

Um . . . well, sure,
    Denise says.
    I guess so. Now?

Yeah, sure,
    I say.

Fifteen minutes later,
>   Denise knocks.

C'mon in,
>   I say.

We go into the kitchen.

I turn on the radio.

Want a Pop-Tart?
>   I ask,
>   opening the cupboard
>   next to the stove.
>   *We have strawberry and . . .*
>   *I guess that's it. Strawberry.*

Hmmm, no thanks,
>   says Denise.
>   *I don't eat that stuff anymore.*

I put the Pop-Tarts
>   back in the
>   cupboard.

Sooooo, tell me!
> Denise says.
> *I heard you got them to change their minds.*
> *Aren't you excited?*

I was,
> I say.
> *But there's been a change of plans.*

What happened?
> asks Denise.
> *I thought you got enough people to sign.*

I did get enough,
> I say.
> *But it's not happening.*

Why not?
> Denise asks.

I really don't want to talk about it,
> I say.

Denise raises her eyebrows.

Okay, sure,
> she says.

But it's probably just as well,
> *she goes on.*
> *Now you can relax.*
> *Have some fun, Grace!*

I guess,
> I say.

What about the rest of the summer?
> *Now that you can't go to camp?*
> Denise asks.

I don't know,
> I say.
> *I haven't really thought about it.*

I'm taking baton twirling,
> Denise gushes,
> *It's soooo groovy!*
> *You should try it, Grace!*

Maybe,
> I say.

Denise starts talking then.

    About Kevin.
        And parties.

    And Kevin.
        And the beach.

    And Kevin.
        And Kevin.
            And Kevin.
                And Kevin.
                    And Kevin.

Well, I need to go,
    she says finally.
Mom says I have to clean my room.
Before Kevin comes over.

She giggles.

Nice seeing you, Grace.

Yeah, I say.
You, too.

She slips out
>   through the garage door and
>   I watch her go.

Wonder when/if
>   I'll see her again.

Wonder if/when
>   we can ever go back
>   to how things were.

For all I know
Denise is right.
Why should I
put up a fight?

Forget the stars.
Forget the moon.
I wish I could
go back to June.

And start this summer
once again.
Go to parties,
hang with friends.

No more dorks and
no more nerds.
Excellent grades are
for the birds.

From now on
I'll keep my peace.
And twirl batons
with cool Denise.

I'M SITTING ON THE FRONT STEP

Watching ants
    build a hill in a
    sidewalk crack.

Mom's at work.

Cyndy's still sleeping.

Dougie never called back.

I look up.

See Mrs. Frost and Celeste
    out for their
    morning walk.

When does your camp start, Grace?
    Mrs. Frost calls.
    You must be excited!

I get up to pet Celeste.

She licks my hand.

I don't look at Mrs. Frost.

I just keep patting Celeste.

Blinking fast to
    clear the
    tears that
    appear.

Well,
    I say.
    About that.

I tell her about Mrs. Green's mom.

I don't really care anymore, anyway,
    I say.
    It's just too much trouble.

Mrs. Frost listens quietly.

I'm sorry, Grace,
    she says when I finish.

Then she points to the sky.

See that, Grace?
> she says.
>> *That's the last bit of the waning crescent moon.*

I look up and—
> even though it's daytime—
> I do see it.

A faint white sliver.

Like an X-ray of the
> moon that
> mocked me
> the other night.

The waning crescent phase was a time to reflect,
> Mrs. Frost says.
> *Let go of things you can't control.*
> *Now, when the new moon comes, you'll be ready.*

Think about it, Grace,
> she says, smiling.

Then she pats me
        on the shoulder.
Continues down the sidewalk
        with Celeste.

I watch them go.

My mind is spinning.

Because I may not know
        anything about the
        phases of the moon.

But I DO know this:

        I have worked
            WAY
            TOO
            HARD
        to give up now.

DOUGIE CALLS AROUND 2:00

Sorry I had to hang up like that,
    he says.
        My mom needed the phone.
        Want to get ice cream?

I'm still a little
    mad about
    yesterday.

But I do love
    ice cream.

Five minutes later,
    we're walking to
    Baskin-Robbins.

How were your grandparents?
    I ask,
    licking my cone.
It's Blue Moon,
    like always.

They're fine,
    Dougie says.
    They're glad we live so close now.

He catches a
>	scoop of mint chip
>	just before it slides off.

All my relatives are in Indiana,
>	I say.
>	*We usually visit them in July.*

Dougie nods.

But Mom says we'll wait this summer,
>	I say.
>	*Until Dad gets home.*

Grace, look,
>	he says.
>	*I'm really sorry about Space Camp.*
>	*Can't your mom go in Mrs. Green's place?*

I thought of that,
>	I say.
>	*But it has to be a teacher.*
>	*I don't have anyone else to ask.*

I understand,
says Dougie.

I stop licking my cone.
Look straight at Dougie.

However, I say.
    I just had an idea.

What's your idea?
    Dougie asks.

What if . . .
    I begin, and he leans in.

What if I put on my own space camp?

I DECIDE TO WAIT

until after the news
        to talk to Mom
        about my idea.

Right at the
        end of the broadcast,
        there's a report on
        Apollo 11.
Perfect.

Speaking of Apollo 11,
        I begin.

I tell her
        what I'm thinking.

Interesting,
        she says
        when I finish.
        You want to do that here?
        At our house?

I'll do all the work,
        I say.
        You'd just have to oversee things.

Let me sleep on it,
    Mom says.

She reaches for
    her newspaper.

We'll need to start planning soon!
    I say.

I raise my eyebrows,
    give her my best smile.

She smiles, too.

It would be kind of like having a party, wouldn't it?
    she says softly.
It's been a long time since we've had a party.

And when I look at her
    up close,
        I see
        just the
        tiniest
        hint of
            sparkle
            in her eyes.

I'M SITTING AT THE KITCHEN TABLE

Planning out my
    space camp.
Fingers crossed and
    hoping for the best.

Mom's getting ready for work.

Don't forget to think about it!
    I say.

She kisses the top of my head.

How could I forget?
    she laughs.
    I want to talk with Mrs. Frost.
    She might like to help.

I'll have an answer for you tonight,
    Mom says.
    Promise.

She's going to say yes.

I can just tell.

AFTER THE NEWS

Mom walks over to
      Mrs. Frost's house.
She's gone for a
      long
        time.

I get antsy.

What if Mom decides
      it's just too much
      right now?

Finally I hear the
      squeak of a door.
Mrs. Frost's voice.

I see her and Mom
      standing on her porch.

Talking.

Nodding.

Mom makes her way
across the lawn.

Well?
> I say.

Let's do it!
> Mom says.
> *Let's have your camp at our house!*

I jump up,
> hug Mom so hard
> I almost
> knock her over.

Mrs. Frost will help,
> Mom says.
> *She said we can watch everything on her TV.*
> *It's a lot bigger than ours.*
> *And it's in color!*

I hug Mom again.

Thank you, Mom,
> I say.
> *Thank you so much.*

Mom just laughs.

It'll be fun.
>	she says.
>	*And Grace?*

What?
>	I say.

This is going to be the greatest space camp ever!
>	Mom says.

>	And I believe her.

I SLEEP LATE THE NEXT MORNING

Cyndy's finishing
    breakfast
        when I come out.

The dork called,
    she says.
    He said to meet him behind the bowling alley.
    At noon.
    He needs to talk to you about
    something important.

What is it?
I ask.

Cyndy just looks at me.
Rolls her eyes.

At noon,
    I pedal over
    to the bowling alley.

Dougie comes out
    just as I ride up.

I lean my bike
        on a tree,
           join him under
           the picnic shelter.

I give him the update.

That's a great plan,
        he says.

Would you like to come?
        I ask him.

Me? To your space camp?
        he asks.
        You mean it's not "girls only"?

Nope! Anyone can come to my camp,
        I say.

Then I'll be there,
        says Dougie.

There's only one thing missing,
        I say.

What's that?
        Dougie asks.

We won't have a NASA scientist speaking,
>   I say.
>   *Brodie must have connections in high places.*

Dougie crumples his lunch bag.

Stands up.

Like he's ready to
>   go back to work.

But he doesn't.
Not right away.

That's what I wanted to talk to you about, Grace,
>   he says.
>   *That NASA scientist?*

Yeah? What about him?

Well,
>   Dougie says.
>   *First of all, it's not a "him."*

I stare at Dougie,
>   shake my head.

What are you talking about?
    I say.
    Of course it is!
    How would you know, anyway?

Well, because . . .

He takes a deep breath.

That NASA scientist is . . . my mom.

I just stare at him.

What?
    I say.
    No way!

It's true,
    Dougie says.
    It's kind of a long story.

I'm just staring at Dougie
    shaking my head.

Then I start to laugh.

Dougie does, too.

Soon tears are
> running down our faces.

He takes off his glasses,
> wipes his eyes.

Does Brodie know?
> I finally gasp.

No, but he will soon,
> Dougie says.
> *She's calling him today.*
> *Telling him she won't speak at his camp.*
> *Not if girls can't go.*

I still can't believe what I'm hearing.

Why didn't you tell me this before?
> I ask.

I wanted to,
> he says.
> *But Mom was waiting for clearance from NASA.*

I almost slipped up a couple of times,
> he says.
> *Like that day at the beach? When the storm hit?*

Brodie's going be so mad,
    I say.

Poor Brodie,
    Dougie says.

Yeah, poor Brodie,
    I say.

But I'm smiling a little.

Well, back to work,
    Dougie says.

I jump on my bike,
    ride home,
        humming all the way.

It has been a VERY
    strange summer.

But right now?

Strange
feels
GREAT.

MOM COMES IN

Her arms are full of
> groceries.

You are NOT going to believe what happened,
> I say.

I launch into the
> story about
> Dougie's mom.

Don't tell anyone yet,
> I say.
> *She still needs to talk to Brodie.*

Mom opens the cupboard.
Pulls out her pills.

I won't tell,
> Mom says.
> *I'm really glad you have a new friend.*
> *Dougie seems like a nice kid.*

Mom stares at
> the pill bottle
> for a few seconds.

Then she puts it back
> in the cupboard.

Things are looking up, Grace,
> she says.

Yes,
> I say.
> *They are.*

THE MOON WALK

is still a few days away.

But today,
>the Apollo 11 rocket
>launches from
>Cape Kennedy
>in Florida.

Dougie invites me over to
>watch with him and
>his family.

I'm really nervous
>now that I know
>about his mom.

But Mom and Cyndy
>are at work.

This will be much better than
>watching alone.

Dougie's mom
        answers the door.

Call me Doreen!
        she says.

The she gives me a hug.

Dougie's dad
        offers me some
        freeze-dried peaches.

Doreen picked this up at work before we moved,
        he says.
It's the same stuff the astronauts have.

I look at him to see if he's
        kidding.

He's not.

I sit on the floor with
        Dougie's little sister,
        Darla.

Dougie gets close to the screen.
Points out the parts
    of the Saturn V rocket.

I look around the room.

I can't believe I'm watching the
    Apollo 11 launch
    with an
    actual NASA scientist.

And HER family.

The *low, steady, calm* news guy
    is reporting.

5, 4, 3, 2, 1, 0 . . .
All engines running!
    a radio crackles.
    Liftoff on Apollo 11!

Even the *low, steady, calm* guy
    sounds excited.

What a moment!
    he says.
    Man on the way to the moon!

Hooray!
    shouts Darla.

Beautiful!
    says Doreen.

She smiles at me.

Someday this will be you, Grace,
    she says quietly.

When I get ready to leave,
    Doreen comes over.
Puts her hands
    on my shoulders.

Listen, Grace,
    she says.
    I can tell you have what it takes to do this.
    Don't give up.

I smile back.
A warm feeling
    fills my chest.
Spreads up to my face.

Thank you,
>I whisper.
>>*Thank you so much.*

I slip my shoes on.

Oh! And Grace?
>Doreen says.
Do you know of a space camp I might be able to visit?

She winks.

So much to do
to set the scene!
I sweep the porch.
The bathroom's clean.

Mom has gathered
up some books.
She's setting up a
reading nook.

Mrs. Frost—
who's very wise—
will serve us all
homemade moon pies.

Even Cyndy
joins the team.
It's like I'm living
in a dream!

This camp is going to
be the best!
But now it's time
to get some rest.

I WAKE UP AT 5:00 A.M.

The sky is glowing
    pink and peach
    with the sunrise.

I'm WAY too excited
    for sleep.

I go over my lists.
    ✓ check
    ✓ check
    ✓ check

My space camp
    is
    READY
    FOR
    LIFTOFF.

DOUGIE AND DARLA

show up first
      with a few of
        Darla's friends.

Then the kids from
      around the corner
      arrive.

Mrs. Frost comes
      across the lawn.
She has a poster showing
      the phases of the moon.

Celeste trots along
      behind her.

At the last minute,
      one of Denise's pals
      from that day
      at the beach
      slips in.

Gives me a tiny wave.

A sheepish smile.
Are you ready?
    I say.
        Space Camp countdown starts now!

10, 9, 8, 7, 6 . . .

Everyone counts together.
5, 4, 3, 2, 1 . . .

BLASTOFF!
Darla and her friends yell.

And just like that,
my space camp
begins.

DOUGIE SHOWS US HIS MODEL

of the Apollo 11 rocket.

Describes all the parts
    and what they do.

Feel free to take a closer look,
    he says.

Everyone claps.

Dougie takes a little bow.
Pushes his glasses up.

Mrs. Frost is next.

It turns out she knows
    even more about the
    moon phases
    than I realized.

Tonight we'll see the waxing crescent moon,
    she says,
        It looks a little like your thumbnail.

She holds up her thumb.

And it happens when . . .

Everyone listens carefully.

They clap for her, too.

Next up is Cyndy.

Two days ago, she
        cornered me in
        the kitchen.

At first I thought she was
        mad at me.

I want to lead that moon phases experiment,
        she said.
            The one in the basement.

I just stared at her.

Okay!
    I said, finally.
Trying not to sound
    TOO surprised.

And here we are.

We press up against the damp walls.

Cyndy circles around a
    lightbulb with a
    baseball.

I'm the earth,
    Cyndy says.
    The baseball is the moon.
    And the lightbulb is the sun.

I get it!
    says Darla.
So cool,
    say the neighbor kids.

We climb
> back up the stairs.
Blinking in the
> bright sunlight.

Doreen has arrived and
> is talking to Mom.
She's the last speaker
> before lunch.

I'm so happy to be here,
> she begins.

Then she tells us about
> the college classes
> she took.

How she got her job at NASA.

I knew I could do it,
> she says.
> *I just had to convince them.*

I'm smiling so hard
         my face hurts.

I can't believe we've pulled this off!

It's a perfect day.

SIMPLY.
PERFECT.

LUNCHTIME!

calls Mom.

Everyone scurries over to
      the faucet by the patio
      to wash their hands.

They're laughing.

Having fun.

It really *is* a little bit like
      a party.

I just stand back and
      watch.

Pinch myself.

Still wondering
      if I'm
         dreaming.

THE DAY FLIES BY

We're surprised it's
    2:30 already when
    Mom calls us over to
    Mrs. Frost's house.

It's almost time for the lunar module
    to land on the moon.

The moon walk will happen
    later tonight.

I'm wedged between
    Cyndy and Dougie
    on the couch.

I'm jiggling my leg and
    Cyndy slaps my knee.

Dougie laughs.

Shhh,
    says Darla.
    I can't hear.

Fourteen minutes to touchdown . . .
>the newscaster says.

Eagle, Houston,
>a voice crackles over the radio.
>*You are go to continue . . .*

And the earth right out our front window,
>says one of the astronauts.

I have goosebumps.

Crowds all over the world are watching and listening,
>says the news guy.

Thirty seconds,
>the radio crackles.

Contact light,
>says the astronaut.
>*Okay, engine stopped . . .*

We watch.

Wait.

Hold our breath.

The Eagle has landed!
    the astronaut finally says.

Everyone else jumps up.

Cheers!

Claps!!

Laughs!!!

But I sit
    quiet
    on the couch
    staring at the TV.

What a miracle,
    I whisper.

What a miracle.

MOM ORDERS PIZZAS FOR DINNER

Mrs. Frost serves her
    moon pies
    for dessert.

We play tag
    in the yard until
    it's too dark to see.

We're sticky with
    marshmallows and
    chocolate and
    sweat when
    we squeeze ourselves into
    Mrs. Frost's living room again.

This part feels
    different.

I think about Dad.

Wonder if he's watching, too.

The TV picture is
        blurry.

We squint to
        make out the
        fuzzy,
        shadowy
        images of the
        astronauts.

They back out of the hatch.

Make their way
        down the ladder
                rung
                      by
                              rung
                                  by
                                        rung

                          on to the
                          moon's
                          dusty surface.

We sit perfectly still as
    we watch the astronauts
      perform their tests.

Conduct their experiments.

Collect their rocks.

We watch them plant a
    little American flag
    in the lunar powder.

It's past midnight by the time they
    start back up the ladder

                                  close the hatch

                              rung

                   by

            rung

      by

rung

And
just
like
that,
it's
over.

No one cheers this time.

No one claps.

No one moves.

We just sit.

Silent.

Full of
wonder.

Awe.

Finally, someone coughs.

Breaks the spell.

We get up slowly,
　　　　groaning,
　　　　　　stretching.

We stand in the yard.

Talk quietly.

Thank you, Mrs. Frost,
    I say.

We'll talk more, Grace,
    says Doreen.

I'll call you,
    says Dougie.

I turn to Mom.

Thank you,
    I say.

You're welcome, honey,
    Mom says.
It was a good day. A very good day.

Her voice catches.

I look up.

Take a quick breath in.

Mom is crying.

IT'S A WARM SUMMER NIGHT

But I'm not small anymore.

Mom and Cyndy and I
    lie side by side
      in the cool grass.

Study the sky.

We even spot a
    shooting star.

I think about the wish
    I made with Dad
    a long time ago.

It's like we touched the moon,
    I murmur.

I think we're gonna make it,
    says Cyndy, softly.

I think so, too,
    whispers Mom.

        And I believe it.

It's not like
everything is groovy.
That just happens
in the movies.

I miss Denise.
I fret for Mom.
Dad is still in
Vietnam.

But lots of good things
happened, too.
I learned that people
do come through!

I learned to work for
what is right.
How not to quit
without a fight.

And even though things
might change soon?
I'll always know
I touched the moon.

Want to Keep Reading?

Here's a sneak peek at another book from West 44 Books:

Tell Me Why the Jack Pine Grows
by D. J. Brandon

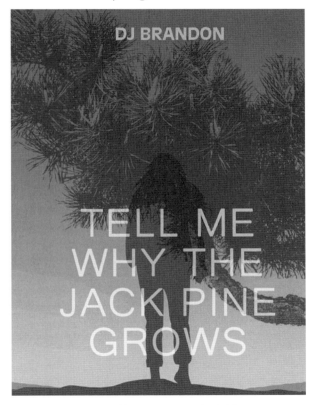

ISBN#: 9781978597242

AT THE RAVINE

Gray rock walls
and jagged ledges
tower above
the creek.

It is a quiet place.
A lonely place.

But to the young jack pine,
it's *home*.

Outward. Upward.
The twisted sapling
reaches.
Stretching toward
the l i g h t . . .

On its own.
Small.
Alone.
On the wall
        of
                  silver
                                  stone.

I KNOW THE JACK PINE WELL

It is my kindred spirit.
    Out of place.
Abandoned
    by the wayward wind
    that brought it here.

I'm standing in the creek bed
far below.
    Squinting
    into sunlight.
    Watching as my older brother, Clay,
    and his friend Caleb
    scale the wall.

I should be with them.
    I wish I was.
    But   B
    I can't
    make   M
    myself
                I

        L

 C

IT'S BECAUSE OF WHAT HAPPENED

when I was six.

Every time
I stand here,
I feel it all
       again.

I look up.
And it
washes
over me.

I feel my foot
slip
on slick,
       mossy
   rocks.

Bits of shale
crumble
in my fingertips.

The sky
shakes.
       And . . .

I am
        f
        a
        l
        l
        i
        n
        g
        .
        .
        .

You'll climb again someday,
    Dad said.
When you've grown up a bit.

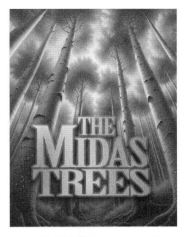
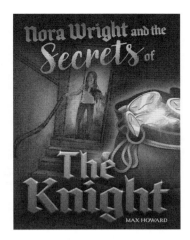

CHECK OUT MORE BOOKS AT:
www.west44books.com

ABOUT THE AUTHOR

Beth Hollar Gier grew up along the eastern shore of Lake Michigan. She studied music at the University of Michigan and worked with middle school and high school students for many years. Beth then earned her MFA in Writing for Children and Young Adults from Hamline University. These days, she lives and writes in Michigan, serves as a mentor for the Minnesota Prison Writing Workshop, and cherishes time with her family. *It's Like We Touched the Moon* is her debut novel. To find out more, visit www.bethgier.com.